# Miaow!

## A Lift the Cat-Flap Book

Allan Ahlberg

illustrated by André Amstutz

WALKER BOOKS
AND SUBSIDIARIES
LONDON · BOSTON · SYDNEY

Clara has a little cat,
A tabby tom named Jack,
And when he goes out for a walk
She waits till he comes back.

She sits there in her easy chair
And reads her easy book
And hears a scratching at the door
And runs to take a look.

She curls up in her easy chair
And watches her TV.
Is that a tapping at the door?
She rushes off to see.

Clara has a little cat,
She loves him best of all,
And every time she hears a noise
She runs into the hall.

She waits up till the stars come out,
The moon is hanging low,
Clouds gather then to fill the sky
And, suddenly, there's snow!

She dozes in her easy chair
And time moves on – tick, tock!

Is that some *singing* she can hear?
And what was that – a knock?

The Seven Dwarfs, whatever next?
A *party* – yes, that's what.

There's sausage rolls and sandwiches
And mince pies piping hot.

Then, when the party's over
And the guests are warm and fed,

They wave bye-bye to Clara
And hurry home to bed.

But Clara has a little cat,
A tabby tom named Jack,
And *always* when he stays out late
She waits … till he comes back.

The End